Smart Mulan

Words and Art by J. Drumm
Final Decision Maker: Gabriela

Cover Design: Donna Cunningham

Smart Princess Books and More Publishing
www.smartprincesses.com

There once was a girl named Mulan, you may have heard she could fight like a boy.

But the truth is that to Mulan, exercising her brain was her biggest joy.

When Mulan was little, she was told that girls couldn't do the same things that boys could do.

But Mulan wouldn't accept this, she knew she had unlimited potential and that you do too!

Just like Mulan your mind is mighty, and there is power in your soul.

You can overcome any challenge,
you can achieve any goal!

As she grew up, Mulan didn't let anything stop her from exploring all sorts of interesting things.

She rode horses, shot arrows, studied engineering, and made music with strings.

But above all that, she cared for all living things and knew about feelings and emotions.

She believed that kindness was an amazing way to solve all kinds of commotions.

She could see and understand how others were feeling because of something called empathy.

She used this to help everyone, not just friends but also any so-called enemy.

When she saw someone sad, mad, or embarrassed, she tried to help that person improve the way they were feeling.

She helped people see that our brains are amazing and can also help others start healing.

Then one day, the news came that armies were getting ready to fight and every family must send a man.

Mulan knew fighting was not the answer and quickly came up with a plan.

She pretended to be a boy so she could be the one sent off to fight.

And she wasted no time in showing the other soldiers it wasn't only muscles that had might.

Yes, at times she had to defend herself and help protect the others that were also sent to fight.

But she wasn't afraid to tell everyone that there were other options that were far more polite.

She told them she was female, and taught the generals how they could find a peaceful solution.

She brought both sides together to work on a more friendly resolution.

Solving conflicts is not always easy, but Mulan doesn't stop trying.

She knows that if we use kindness and listen, we can help people that are mad, sad, or even crying.

So by using her brain, Mulan helped her country find a peaceful solution, and everyone stopped fighting.

And just like her you are amazing, your brain is powerful and creative and exciting!

The emperor was quite impressed with the way Mulan used her brain, and so was his son.

And Mulan helped teach the country that solving problems with kindness is best for everyone.

And just like Mulan,
you can use your brain like that too!

You can solve any problem and be successful in whatever you do!

Try hard and learn from your mistakes, and your brain will take you far.

Believe in yourself,
you are great just the way you are!

The Smart Princess Series

John Drumm is a dad and like any parent, he wants his daughter to know she can accomplish anything in life. When his daughter started to adore princesses and they watched the 'classic' movies and read the books, he became concerned. He didn't want her to think she needed a prince to rescue her or that her options were limited. That's how The Smart Princess Series was born. The message is simple: our daughters / loved ones can accomplish anything they want in life.

Honest reviews help other parents and caregivers determine if this story is right for them and their loved ones. Please visit the site where you purchased this book and write a brief review. Thank you!

For information on other stories please visit us at: www.SmartPrincesses.com

Made in the USA
Columbia, SC
08 July 2022